PUFFIN BOO

HAPPY CHRISTMAS
HAMMY
THE WONDER HAMSTER

Bethany brushed her hair and worked her way back towards the stage, glancing from side to side in the hope of catching a glimpse of Hamilton. Parents were taking their seats and leafing through their programmes. Children were in organized groups of stars, angels, snowflakes, robins and carol singers. She slipped her hand into her pocket, hoping desperately that Hamilton might have jumped back in without her noticing, but there was nothing there except a tissue and a pound coin.

Hamilton! Please! she thought. *Where are you?*

Have you read all of Hammy's adventures?

HAMMY THE WONDER HAMSTER

HAPPY CHRISTMAS, HAMMY THE
WONDER HAMSTER

POPPY HARRIS

HAPPY CHRISTMAS HAMMY THE WONDER HAMSTER

PUFFIN

PUFFIN BOOKS

Published by the Penguin Group
Penguin Books Ltd, 80 Strand, London WC2R 0RL, England
Penguin Group (USA) Inc., 375 Hudson Street, New York, New York 10014, USA
Penguin Group (Canada), 90 Eglinton Avenue East, Suite 700, Toronto, Ontario, Canada M4P 2Y3
(a division of Pearson Penguin Canada Inc.)
Penguin Ireland, 25 St Stephen's Green, Dublin 2, Ireland (a division of Penguin Books Ltd)
Penguin Group (Australia), 250 Camberwell Road, Camberwell, Victoria 3124, Australia
(a division of Pearson Australia Group Pty Ltd)
Penguin Books India Pvt Ltd, 11 Community Centre, Panchsheel Park, New Delhi – 110 017, India
Penguin Group (NZ), 67 Apollo Drive, Rosedale, North Shore 0632, New Zealand
(a division of Pearson New Zealand Ltd)
Penguin Books (South Africa) (Pty) Ltd, 24 Sturdee Avenue, Rosebank, Johannesburg 2196, South Africa

Penguin Books Ltd, Registered Offices: 80 Strand, London WC2R 0RL, England

puffinbooks.com

First published 2009
1

Text copyright © Poppy Harris, 2009
Extracts from 'How Far is it to Bethlehem?' by Frances Chesterton appear on pp. 80–82
All rights reserved

The moral right of the author has been asserted

Typeset in 13.75/20.5pt Bembo by Palimpsest Book Production Limited,
Grangemouth, Stirlingshire
Made and printed in England by Clays Ltd, St Ives plc

British Library Cataloguing in Publication Data
A CIP catalogue record for this book is available from the British Library

ISBN: 978-0-141-32484-5

www.greenpenguin.co.uk

Penguin Books is committed to a sustainable future
for our business, our readers and our planet.
The book in your hands is made from paper
certified by the Forest Stewardship Council.

To Thomas and James

chapter 1

'Now that it's December, Hamilton, we might have snow,' said Bethany as she looked down from her bedroom window. 'It'll be beautiful. I hope it snows soon.'

Hamilton, her white and gold hamster, had perched on the windowsill. He looked up as if hoping to see a few soft flakes twirl down from the sky. Hamilton had never seen snow apart from in pictures and on television, but he was looking forward to seeing it for real.

Hamilton was no ordinary hamster. He had chosen his own name, for a start. Some people, like Bethany's little brother Sam, called him Hammy, but Bethany always used his proper name. He knew whole books full of information. He understood speech in hundreds of languages (including Rabbit). He knew all about mathematics, computers and engineering, and was particularly interested in aeroplanes. One thing he didn't know was how he came to be so intelligent. He didn't know that he had a tiny microchip – a microspeck – stuck in his cheek pouch.

It had happened like this. A brilliant young scientist called Tim Taverner had made the microspeck for putting artificial intelligence into a computer, but it had been accidentally thrown into a waste-paper basket and ended up in some hamster bedding. Hamilton's hamster bedding. So the artificial intelligence hadn't gone into a computer at all. It had gone into Hamilton, and he was making very good use of it.

Only Bethany and Hamilton knew how brilliant he was. They felt it was best to keep it secret, even from Bethany's best friend Chloe.

Bethany shook her dark hair back from her face. 'I went out for school in a hurry today,' she said. 'I didn't open my advent calendar. Do you want to help?'

With Hamilton's claw and Bethany's fingernail, they opened the tiny cardboard door. Behind it was a picture of a curvy white figure with snowflakes all around it. Hamilton looked more closely with his head on one side and decided it was a number eight wearing a hat.

'It's a snowman,' said Bethany, and picked Hamilton up. 'You make a snowball and roll it round and round in more snow until it's big enough for the body, then make a smaller one for the head.'

Hamilton balanced neatly on her fingertips and stretched to get a better look at the picture. Yes, he could see how it was done. If people could make snowmen, he'd like to have a go at making a snow hamster.

For the last week or two, Bethany had been telling him about Christmas – there was a lot to learn. First of all there was Mary, Joseph, Jesus and the stable.

Hamilton had looked very carefully at pictures of Mary, Joseph and Jesus, and was surprised, and a little indignant. Where was the hamster? There must surely have been hamsters in Bethlehem in those days. They probably would have lived in the desert, and so could have followed the Three Wise Men – but nobody ever seemed to put one in the Nativity scene. There were donkeys, camels, sheep, cows, sometimes dogs, and perhaps even a mouse, but never a hamster. He had used Bethany's phone to text her a question – Y IS THERE NO HMSTR IN STABLE?

Bethany had thought for a moment. 'I expect it's hiding in the manger,' she had said. 'It's keeping the baby company.' That had sounded perfectly reasonable to Hamilton. Maybe the hamster had given itself to the baby as a present.

But all the Christmas information didn't stop there. Oh no. There were presents, and somebody called Father Christmas or Santa Claus. There were parties, decorations, cards, holly, carol singing, special things to eat, grannies, uncles who fell asleep in front of the television and even more presents. Oh, and there were crackers, except that these crackers weren't something to eat – and they didn't crack, they banged and had presents inside. Amazing! Children could even hang up a sock, and find it filled with little presents in the morning – except that at Christmas it wasn't called a sock, it was called a stocking. It was all very exciting.

That reminded him – what could he give Bethany for Christmas? He climbed on to her phone.

WHAT WOULD U LIKE MOST OF ALL 4 CHRISTMAS? he texted.

Bethany smiled and stroked him. 'I'd love to have snow,' she said. 'Lots of snow, on Christmas Day. That's called a white Christmas, but it hardly ever happens.'

It might happen this year, thought Hamilton. If Bethany wanted snow for Christmas, there must be some way of getting it for her. It wouldn't be easy, but he would enjoy the challenge. *There must be a way* . . . He was thinking hard about this as Bethany turned at last from the window and picked up a small, flat pillowcase. Not being sure what it was for, he twitched his nose and whiskers at it and looked at her with his head on one side.

'I'm decorating a cushion cover,' Bethany said, smiling at Hamilton's inquisitive expression. 'I'm making it for Chloe, as a Christmas present. I know it doesn't look much yet, but I'm going to put ribbons across it, and write her name with fabric pens, then I'll fill it with stuffing to make it soft.'

She saw the surprise on his face, and added quickly, 'That's a kind of soft, fluffy material, Hamilton. It's not the stuffing you put in a Christmas turkey.'

Hamilton was extremely glad to hear it. He climbed up on to the cushion and decided that Chloe would be getting a very special Christmas present. And she wouldn't be the only one. Somehow, Bethany would get her wish.

chapter 2

The next morning, when everybody was out, Hamilton was on a mission. He searched all round Bethany's bedroom, then he scurried across the landing to her little brother Sam's room but still couldn't find what he was looking for. Finally, he ran to Mum and Dad's room and found in the waste-paper basket the very thing he wanted – a newspaper!

Hamilton loved newspapers. He read quickly through the stories, did the Sudoku and the crossword in his head, then turned to what he really needed – the weather forecast.

Unfortunately, it was most disappointing. The forecaster said that there would be snow before Christmas and snow after Christmas, but that Christmas itself would be green, not white. There wouldn't be a single snowflake, an icicle or even a touch of frost on Christmas Day.

Hamilton didn't like that forecast at all. With any luck, the forecaster had got it wrong. There was a television in the room with the remote control lying on a low table, just where he could reach it. Hopefully, he flicked through the channels and found a programme with three boring people sitting on a settee talking nonsense, a cartoon that he found very silly and a man painting a front door, then, finally, he found a weather forecast.

The weathergirl was smiley and cheerful, but she didn't give Hamilton any hope. She said that it would be too wet for snow, then too warm, then it would be very cold, but the wrong sort of cold for snow.

'There may be *some* snow in December,' she said at last, 'but I'm afraid we're not expecting a white Christmas this year.'

Hamilton stood on the remote to switch it off and glared at the television. If Bethany wanted a white Christmas she would have one. All that was needed was an intelligent hamster and something as snowy as possible.

A box of cotton-wool bobbles sat on the little table on Mum's side of the bed. That would make a good start! Hamilton tugged one from the box and scampered back to Bethany's room with it, where he tucked it behind the wardrobe. He'd never seen anyone do any cleaning there, so it would be safe. One bobble would make – oh, about five snowflakes, he thought.

While Hamilton was planning a white Christmas for Bethany, somebody else was making plans too. In the city was a university, and in the university was a laboratory with computers, microscopes and gleaming white boxes with flashing lights. Watching the computer screens, a thin young man with messy dark hair sat in a black leather office chair, swivelling from side to side and chewing the end of a pencil.

The young man was Dr Tim Taverner, the brilliant scientist who had accidentally dropped the microspeck into the waste-paper basket with his sandwich crumbs, which had resulted in Hamilton becoming the most super-intelligent hamster ever. Tim had found out that the paper from his waste-paper basket had been taken to Dolittle's Pet Shop to be used as hamster bedding, and had tried to get the speck back – but by the time he got there, the microspeck was in Hamilton, and Hamilton was in Bethany's bedroom. Tim hadn't given up, though. A lot of the work he was doing was secret and strictly against the law, and he mustn't be found out. So Tim had made a tracking device to home in on the speck, and had discovered that the hamster belonged to either the dark-haired girl at Number 33 Tumblers Crescent (Bethany) or her blonde friend across the road (Chloe).

He'd even tried to kidnap Hamilton, and failed. Now, Christmas was coming. He'd soon be going away to his parents' house, but he was so determined to get on with his work and to catch the hamster that he didn't want to leave until he really, really had to – say, on Christmas Eve. He didn't much like being at home because he got bored there, but his mum did cook a magnificent Christmas dinner.

He stopped swivelling his chair and looked at his diary. There were still two weeks and a few days to go before Christmas. 'I must get that hamster,' he muttered to himself. Two or three times a week he drove down Tumblers Crescent, looking out for any opportunity to

get Hamilton back. He couldn't go away
without one more try.

There was suddenly an unpleasant taste of
wood and rubber in his mouth. He'd chewed
the top of his pencil right off.

chapter 3

That afternoon, Hamilton woke up suddenly at
ten to four. He always woke up at ten to four on
school days, because that was when Bethany and
her brother Sam came home. On this particular
afternoon, he could hear three pairs of feet
hurrying up the stairs, and an extra voice.

That's Chloe, he thought. He liked Chloe,
even though she talked a lot of nonsense to him
and – he didn't like to think about this – called
him Fluffpot. Chloe was Bethany's best friend,
which made her a Nice Person. He always
looked forward to his after-school chat with

Bethany, but that would have to wait until Chloe had gone home.

Bethany and Chloe tumbled excitedly into the room, dropped their school bags, threw their coats on the bed and then bounced on it. From the bounce and their bright eyes, Hamilton knew that something special was going on.

'Hello, Hamilton!' called Bethany, as Chloe dashed home to get changed. As soon as she had gone, Hamilton opened his cage. He jumped on to Bethany's hands and rubbed his face against her thumb.

'We're doing a Christmas end-of-term concert at school,' whispered Bethany. 'We always have one, but this year, Miss Fossett asked me to sing a solo. I couldn't! I'd be too scared to sing by myself in front of everyone! So then she asked Chloe to do it, and she was scared too, so we asked if we could sing together, and she said yes!'

The door opened and Chloe appeared.
Bethany was still talking to Hamilton, but
there was nothing strange about this. (It's all
right to be seen talking to your hamster –
Chloe talked to her hamster, Toffee, all the
time. All hamster owners do that. It's only
when the hamster sends text messages back
that some people get alarmed.)

'Did you hear that, little Fluffpot?' said
Chloe. Hamilton couldn't help cringing.
This was the 127th time she'd called him that.
'Bethany and I are going to sing in the concert!'

Hamilton couldn't understand why Bethany
didn't want to sing by herself. He'd heard her
singing while she got dressed in the mornings,
ran up and down stairs and listened to the
music on her iPod, and she had a lovely voice.
As Bethany and Chloe chatted about what
they had to sing, and whether they'd have to
wear school uniform, Hamilton jumped into
his wheel and checked that Chloe wasn't

looking while he adjusted the gears before
going for a run.

Other hamsters might have been happy just
to run on the wheel, but to Hamilton, this was
boring. He liked to imagine himself having an
adventure. This time, as he'd been learning
about winter, he decided that he was running
across plains covered in snow, with icy
mountains all around, and through shining frost
tunnels hung with icicles . . .

He was just having a ride on a galloping
polar bear when the door opened. Sam had
one foot across the entrance to his big sister's
room when he remembered that he was
supposed to knock. He went out again,
knocked and waited until Bethany called,
'Come in, Sam!' He entered properly this time,
throwing back the door so hard that Hamilton
felt his wheel rattle.

'You know the school concert?' he asked.

'Yes, we're singing in it!' said Chloe, but

Bethany could see that this wasn't the response Sam had wanted.

'What about the concert, Sam?' she asked.

'I'm in it!' he announced proudly. 'I have to do forward and backward rolls, and star jumps, and all that acrobatic stuff, cos we're doing this dance thing about snow scenes and snowball fights. I got chosen to be the snowball!'

'So the snowball does star jumps and forward rolls?' said Bethany.

'Yeah, when it's flying through the air,' said Sam. 'I'm best at gymnastics, so I got chosen for that.'

'That's great, Sam!' said Bethany. 'Well done!'

'I'm going to practise,' he announced, and ran out, and soon there were thumps and bumps from the landing as he practised his acrobatics before hammering down the stairs and going outside to the shed to clean out his rabbit's hutch.

Hamilton did a few exercises too, and thought

about snow. He had enough cotton wool now to do about fifty snowflakes. By his calculations, he still needed at least another 4,950, and he wasn't at all sure how to find them.

Each morning, Hamilton and Bethany opened another door on the advent calendar, and each afternoon after school Bethany and Chloe practised their song, sometimes at Chloe's house, sometimes at Bethany's. Hamilton wished he could sing. Soon he knew every note and every word, and conducted with an apple stalk when Chloe wasn't looking. He had a finely tuned ear for music and could read it too. He could even tell if either of the girls sang a little sharp or flat, or missed a beat. One afternoon, when Chloe had gone home after a pretty terrible practice, Bethany sat down heavily on the bed. Hamilton climbed on to her hand.

'It's no good, Hamilton,' sighed Bethany.

'We can't do a thing right, and it's making me nervous. I wish we hadn't said we'd do this.'

Hamilton pawed at her hand for the phone.

U DID IT BETTER YESTERDAY, he texted. I CAN HELP.

'Can you, Hamilton?' asked Bethany. He never stopped surprising her.

IF U SING FLAT, he told her, I'LL GO . . . he tipped his head to the left. AND IF U SING SHARP, I'LL GO . . . he tipped his head to the right. He was adding, BUT YR NRLY PERFECT, as Sam opened the door, shut it again, knocked and came in. He grinned when he saw Hamilton.

'He looks as if he's sending a text,' he said. Hamilton whipped his paw from the keypad and busily washed his whiskers. 'Will you come and watch me do my snowball thing?'

They were watching from the bedroom door while Sam did three somersaults in a row, two forward and one back, when Mum

came up the stairs. She carried a cardboard
box in her arms.

'Sam, it's like having a baby hippopotamus
in the house!' she said. 'Do you have to do
that?'

'I'm practising!' insisted Sam. 'I have to keep
practising!'

'Oh, if it's for the concert, I suppose it's OK,'
she said, but she looked as if she'd be glad when
the concert was over. 'Bethany, you're making a
cushion for Chloe, aren't you?'

'Yes,' said Bethany, 'but I haven't got anything
to –'

'– to stuff it with, I know,' said Mum.
'I went to the wholesalers today, so I bought
some kapok. That's the white fluffy stuff
for filling toys and things. You can use some
of that.'

'Thanks, Mum!' said Bethany as she took the
box. Hamilton peeped inside and saw soft
white fluff.

Snow! he thought. At least, it looked like snow to him.

The next morning, Bethany opened her advent calendar and found a picture of something that looked like a big brown stone with white paint poured over it, but she told Hamilton it was a Christmas pudding. When she had gone to school, he let himself out of his cage. The box of white fluffy kapok was beside her bed, so Hamilton measured the distance, took a run and a jump and landed in it.

What wonderful stuff! He tunnelled into it, rolled in it, burrowed down into it with only his nose and whiskers sticking out and finally remembered what he was meant to be doing. He crammed his cheek pouches with all the kapok he could fit in. He'd need lots of this. Soon, he'd managed to fill the secret corner behind the wardrobe, so he had to start on the suitcase that lived on top of it. Fortunately, it had been left lopsided and had fallen open at one corner.

Bethany's dressing gown came in very useful for reaching the suitcase. She had left it hanging on the wardrobe door, and it gave Hamilton something to climb up. Even so, running up and down the dressing gown was hard work. He had to stop for a ten-minute feed, a five-minute wash and a three-hour nap, then he went on scurrying back and forward with his cheeks bulging and fluff sticking to his nose and ears. He was concentrating so hard that he didn't hear the front door open as Bethany came home. He was halfway up the dressing gown with his pouches brimful of fluff when he heard her running up the stairs, singing her song. He leapt over to his cage and dived head first into his nest box. Bethany opened the door.

'Hello, Hamilton!' she called. He usually came straight to meet her, and she was surprised to have no answer. It made her nervous if he didn't greet her right away.

'Hamilton,' she said softly, 'are you all right?' Hearing strange scrabbling noises coming from the nest box, she knelt down in front of the cage. 'I'm home!'

Hamilton was struggling to empty the stuffing from his pouches into his nest box. It didn't taste nice, so it might not be good for hamsters and it made his nose tickle. He was rubbing his face with his paws when he finally popped up to meet Bethany.

'Have you been asleep?' she said, and lifted him from his cage. 'You're such a sweetie!'

Hamilton didn't like being called a sweetie, but he knew Bethany couldn't help it. He rubbed his face on her hand much harder than usual, to take the tickle out of his nose. There was a thud and a bump on the landing as Sam practised being a snowball. Bethany took out her phone and sat Hamilton in front of it.

'What have you been doing all day?' she asked.

Hamilton shrugged. NOT MUCH, he texted back.

'I'm sure you've done lots of things,' she said. 'Did you have a run?'

YES. He'd done lots of running.

'Have you done anything else?'

His whiskers twitched as if he were smiling.

JST STUFF, he texted.

'That reminds me,' Bethany said, 'I want to finish Chloe's cushion tonight.' She picked up the box of kapok. 'Oh. I thought there was lots more than that! Mum must have used some. But there should just about be enough.'

Hamilton yawned, ran back into his cage and hid in his nest box before Bethany could ask any more awkward questions. Tomorrow would be one more window on the advent calendar and a day nearer to Christmas, and he still needed another 4,200 more snowflakes.

# chapter 4

The next morning, Bethany opened her advent calendar and found a picture of a white dove. It was the dove that made Hamilton think of feathers.

He sat up, washing his whiskers and waiting for Bethany to go to school. And as soon as the house was quiet, he left his cage and jumped on to her roughly made bed.

Running across a soft and lumpy duvet isn't easy for a small animal. Hamilton sank into it at once and couldn't see where he was going, but he was a determined hamster, and with a few jumps he was safely on the pillows. There must be thousands of feathers in those pillows – he'd seen the odd one fall out when Bethany or Mum plumped them up. Feathers would make wonderful snow.

Hamilton was much too sensible to simply chew a big hole in the pillow. Feathers all over the floor wouldn't do. He nibbled delicately at a corner, just enough to pull out a few soft white feathers. He took one, blew it into the air and watched it drift across the bed. He blew it again, and it lifted a little.

Feathers are fun, thought Hamilton. A bookmark lay on Bethany's bedside table, so he picked it up in both paws and fanned furiously. The feather rose in the air, drifted and fell. Hamilton had never seen a real snowflake, but he thought they must look very like this. He tugged out some more feathers and flapped the bookmark until his paws hurt – then he reminded himself that he was supposed to be gathering these feathers, not playing with them. He took one in his mouth and ran back to his nest box.

He did stop for a second when he happened to see his reflection and realized that a hamster with a feather in his mouth looks a bit silly. He was glad there was nobody to see him. Bethany and Chloe would probably have called him cute, but he thought he just looked ridiculous. He avoided the mirror after that. He pushed a few feathers into his nest box and a lot more down the back of the radiator.

Finally, he went back to examine the hole in the pillow and was surprised to see that it was bigger than he'd meant it to be. Bethany always gave it a little shake before she went to bed at night to make it comfortable, and she wouldn't want a feather explosion. Could he mend it? He sat back, considering it. He knew where to find a needle and thread, but his paws wouldn't be able to manage a needle made for human hands. Sewing was out then.

Bethany kept glue in her desk. He could glue the pillow back together — but when he read the instruction on the glue pot he decided it wouldn't be a good idea. Bethany might come home to find a feathery hamster stuck to a glue pot. And what if the glue took a long time to dry? He wouldn't like Bethany to wake up stuck to her pillow. He would have to make do with pulling the edges of the hole together as closely as he could and tucking the nibbled corner neatly over. Then he went back to his cage and burrowed into his nest box.

Feathers make you tired, he thought, as he fell asleep.

He woke as usual at ten to four, feeling exceptionally cosy. He could hear Bethany and Chloe running up the stairs, chatting and laughing, and he came to the bars of the cage to meet Bethany.

'Have you had a lovely day?' she said, and took him from his cage and stroked his back as he rubbed his face against her hand. 'We've had such a fun time!'

'Bibble-bubble!' called Chloe, and fell laughing on the bed.

Listening to their conversation, which didn't always make sense, Hamilton put the story together. Bethany didn't usually like maths, but they had been playing a maths game at school that had actually been quite fun. Starting with 'one', everybody had to say a number in turn, but if the number was a multiple of three, you had to say 'bibble'. A multiple of four was 'bubble' and a number like twelve, which was both, was 'bibble-bubble'. By the time they had taken off their coats Hamilton had worked out the whole sequence up to several million bibbles and bubbles, but Bethany and Chloe were still playing the game.

'It's bibble-bibble-bubble!' gasped Bethany.

'No, it's bubble-bubble-bibble!' began Chloe, and, laughing too much to say any more, grabbed a pillow from the bed.

No, don't! thought Hamilton. Suddenly, the bibble-bubble game was turning into a bubbly-bibbly giggly pillow-fight as Bethany picked up the other pillow with both hands. Hamilton wasn't sure he could look. He squeezed his eyes shut.

Oh, no, Bethany, don't!' he thought. Daring to open one eye, he shook his head as hard as he could, but it was no good. Bethany wasn't looking.

'It's bibble!' laughed Bethany, swinging a pillow at Chloe.

'It's bubble!' shrieked Chloe, hitting back. Hamilton put both paws over his eyes.

When he peeped through his claws, he

couldn't see Bethany and Chloe at all. They were hidden in a swirl of feathers that filled the room from floor to ceiling.

Oops, thought Hamilton. *Sorry.* He really hadn't intended this to happen, but he did think the snowstorm was beautiful, and Bethany looked very pretty as she appeared gradually through the cloud with feathers in her hair. The girls stood in wide-eyed silence, their hands pressed to their mouths, as feathers settled on their heads, their school uniforms, the bed and the floor. Some landed on Hamilton's cage, so he grabbed them and stuffed them in his nest box while nobody was looking. Bethany's cuddly dog, Wimble, was a feathery mound with only his nose sticking out. There was a nervous little giggle from Chloe and a spurt of smothered laughter from Bethany.

'My mum will kill me!' she whispered.

'She doesn't have to find out,' Chloe

whispered back, scooping up a handful of feathers from the bed. 'Quick, we can . . .'

She stopped as the door opened. Mum stood there, staring.

'Bethany!' she exclaimed. 'What is going on here?'

A moment before, Bethany couldn't stop laughing. Now, her legs felt wobbly and she could hardly speak.

'Sorry,' she said, in a very small voice. 'It just – sort of – burst.'

'I can see that,' said Mum. 'I suppose it burst all by itself, without any help?' She took the sagging, half-empty pillow from Chloe's hands and inspected it. 'It could be just old, and the stitching's worn . . .' She looked more closely. 'You haven't made a hole in this on purpose, have you?'

'No!' said Bethany so indignantly that Mum believed her. Mum sighed.

'Sorry. I'll clear it up,' said Bethany.

'Yes, sorry, Mrs Elliott, so will I,' said Chloe.

'Your mum just phoned, Chloe,' said Mum. 'She wants you home now.'

Chloe left with a sad and sympathetic glance towards Bethany, and Mum followed her downstairs. As soon as the door had closed, Hamilton scrambled out of his cage, gathering up a mouthful of feathers and taking them to Bethany.

'Are you helping?' she said, and lifted him on to her hand, holding him against her cheek the way she did when she was sad. As it was his fault that she was sad in the first place, this made him feel even worse. It was no good trying to explain and apologize – he couldn't do that without giving away the secret of Bethany's Christmas present. All he could do was to help tidy up.

Bethany pushed feathers back into the pillow, which only seemed to make the hole bigger, while Hamilton cleared up as many feathers as he could and hid some while Bethany wasn't looking. By teatime, with his help, Bethany had not only cleared up the feathers, but she'd also done her homework, mended the pillow and practised her song.

When she was asleep, Hamilton helped himself to a few tissues from the box beside her bed and some scraps of paper from the waste-paper basket. They'd make good snow when he'd shredded them up.

Every day, when nobody was about, he added to his snow store, but he urgently needed some new supplies. His idea with the feathers had got Bethany into trouble, and now he wasn't sure he could even give her the white Christmas she wanted. At a rough guess, Hamilton still needed about 3,900 snowflakes.

chapter 5

Christmas drew nearer day by day, and
Hamilton had still only half-filled the suitcase.
The day before the concert, Bethany opened
her advent calendar and found a picture of an
angel blowing a long thin trumpet. She gazed
out of the window dreamily.

'Frost!' she suddenly declared.

Hamilton got out of his cage to have a look,
and his eyes widened. Everything sparkled.
A white twinkly blanket covered the ground,
fences and tops of cars. He leant his paws
against the glass to take a better look, and a

little damp condensation from the window clung to his fur.

'Don't stay there getting wet,' Bethany warned. 'You might catch cold.'

Hamilton held out his paw for the phone. U ALWAYS WORRY ABOUT THAT, he told her. I'LL B OK.

'Keep warm,' she insisted. 'Colds can be dangerous for hamsters.'

The minute Bethany had gone to school, Hamilton ran to Mum and Dad's bedroom to look for more cotton-wool bobbles and tissues, but there were hardly any left, and it might look strange if the last ones disappeared. He'd have to search elsewhere. He was running along the landing, twitching his nose hopefully, when he saw a cardboard box that he knew hadn't been there the night before. Christmas decorations was scrawled in felt-tip pen on the side.

Hamilton scrambled up the side of the box

and peered into it. This was worth knowing about! Little chunks of something white were piled high, and Hamilton took one in his paws, turned it round, sniffed it and finally bit into it. Expanded polystyrene! *White* expanded polystyrene! Perfect snow!

He wriggled further down in the box. The Christmas decorations had been carefully packed, so there was lots of polystyrene to collect. He ran backwards and forwards along the landing, storing his new snow in the hiding places until he was yawning.

He was very tired, and when he settled down for a sleep his nest felt softer and warmer than ever. He was still asleep at Bethany's home time, and he might have slept through that if the front door hadn't banged so hard that the whole house trembled.

'Sam!' called Mum. 'What was that for?'

Sam stamped up the stairs without speaking. Hamilton heard him slam his bedroom door,

and there was a thud and a rattle as Sam's
school bag hit the wall. Hamilton let himself
out of his cage and ran on to the landing to
find out what was happening. At the bottom
of the stairs, Bethany was talking to Mum,
and he could tell from her voice that she
was worried.

'It's that dancing snowball thing,' she was
saying. 'They've given him a costume to wear
and he hates it, so now he doesn't want to do it
any more.' Sam emerged from his bedroom
with another shuddering bang of the door.
Hamilton hid behind the door frame.

'Stupid costume!' yelled Sam. He sounded
near to tears. 'I told Miss Fossett that I didn't
want to wear it, but she said if I don't wear the
costume I can't do the dance, and I've practised
and practised. I was looking forward to it!'

There was a choking sound and a sniff from
Sam. Bethany and Mum ran upstairs, and Mum
sat down beside Sam with her arm round his

shoulders. Bethany slipped past them into her bedroom. Hamilton ran after her and she let him jump on to her hand.

'Poor Sam,' she said. 'He was going to do the dance in his PE kit, then Miss Fossett – our Headmistress who teaches music and organizes the concert – found this snowball suit in a cupboard somewhere, which she remembered making years ago. She's thrilled with it, so she made up her mind that Sam should wear it tomorrow. And by the way, Hamilton, he's right. It is a stupid costume.'

Hamilton put out his paw to ask for the phone. WHAT DOES IT LOOK LIKE? he texted.

'It's like a great big tennis ball made of foam,' Bethany said, 'and it's got lots of fluffy sparkly stuff all over it. Honestly, Hamilton,' she leant closer to whisper in his ear, 'Sam mustn't hear this, but he looks like a dollop of mashed potato. Sparkly mashed potato. But Miss Fossett thinks it's wonderful, and once she's got an idea

into her head nobody can get it out again.
Sam's a Year Four boy. Boys don't do dressing
up unless it's monsters or hero stuff. And
snowball costumes aren't monsters or hero stuff.
I wonder how Miss Fossett would like to stand
up in front of all the parents herself, dressed as a
snowball?'

WHERE IS IT? Hamilton asked.

'The costume?' said Bethany. 'It's at school,
ready for the concert.'

If only Sam had brought the costume home,
Hamilton thought to himself. He could have
done something about it then. Bethany's
voice was becoming high and tight, as if she
might cry.

'I'm getting sick of this concert!' she
complained. 'It's all going wrong for Sam, and
now Chloe's got a sore throat so she needs to
rest her voice, and we can't practise tonight.
I wasn't nervous before, but now it's so close.
It's tomorrow night, and I'm terrified. At least

Chloe will be there, so there'll be two of us,
I suppose.'

3 OF US? texted Hamilton and looked up at
her hopefully.

'Of course you can come!' she said, and
stroked him.

Bethany went to bed at the usual time and read
for a while, as she always did. Hamilton sat on
the pillow beside her and read too, until she put
her light out and he went for his nightly run.
She was pleasantly drowsy when the door
opened and Sam stood there, looking very little
in his pyjamas.

'I can't sleep,' he said. 'I was really looking
forward to the concert, and it's spoilt now.'

Bethany moved over so he could wriggle
into bed beside her.

'It isn't spoilt,' she said. 'Really, Sam, it's
going to be all right. I'm not sure how, but it
will. This time tomorrow it will all be over, and

it'll nearly be Christmas. Worrying doesn't
make it better. Now go to bed, and try to think
of something nice.'

Sam scrambled out of Bethany's bed.

'I don't know how you can sleep with that
hamster wheel running,' he said.

'I don't think I could sleep without it,' said
Bethany. She lay down and, lulled by the gentle
whirring of Hamilton's wheel, was soon asleep.
Hamilton stayed wide awake, deep in thought,
looking at the doors on the advent calendar as
he ran. There weren't many left. Where could
he find all those snowflakes?

Hamilton wasn't the only one who stayed
awake that night. Tim Taverner lay in his bed
and wondered how he could trap the Wonder
Hamster. Was it at Bethany's house, or Chloe's?
Could he sneak in pretending to be the
postman or the gasman, or climb up the side of
the house pretending to be Father Christmas?

Could he pretend to be a hamster-sitter, looking after hamsters during the Christmas holidays? No, that wouldn't do. All night in his dreams, he chased hamsters, carol-singing hamsters, hamsters with sacks full of toys and flying hamsters pulling a sleigh. But he couldn't catch a single one.

chapter 6

'Snow!' cried Bethany. 'Look, Hamilton! Snow!'

Hamilton woke up, sniffing the air. It smelt strangely different today. Bethany was swishing the curtains open.

'Snow!' she said again, and leant her elbows on the sill as she watched. 'Real snow too! Look, Hamilton! It'll settle – that means it won't melt straight away, it'll last all day at least, even if we're not going to have a lovely snowy Christmas.'

Hamilton opened his cage and ran out to sit on her hand. As soon as he saw the snow,

he understood exactly why Bethany loved it
so much.

White flakes twirled and danced. They
settled on trees, grass and rooftops. As he
watched, they covered the garden with a thin
white veil.

'Isn't it magical!' whispered Bethany as she
lifted down the advent calendar so Hamilton
could open it. Inside was a picture of a red front
door with a holly wreath hanging up and snow
on the ledges. 'It looks like our front door.'

From Sam's bedroom came a cry of 'Snow,
snow, snow!'. Dad hurried along the landing,
saying something about having to leave for work
early because the snow would slow the traffic
down. Bethany washed and dressed quickly.

By the time Chloe called to walk to school
the snow was falling heavily, and with every
minute the outside world turned whiter.
Bethany pulled on her wellies and wriggled her
hands into fluffy mittens.

'Now, hurry home after school,' said Mum. 'There'll only just be time to eat your tea and get back to school for the concert. Chloe, how's your throat?'

'It's better, thank you,' said Chloe, but her voice was croaky.

'There's barely any point in going in,' said Bethany. 'It's snowing. The concert's tonight, and it's nearly the end of term. We won't do any work.'

Chloe sneezed.

'Bless you!' said everyone. Now that she looked properly, Bethany saw that Chloe's eyes looked pink and tired.

'Are you all right?' she asked.

'I'm fine,' said Chloe. 'The snow makes my eyes water.'

As soon as the children had gone to school and Mum had shut herself in the sewing room, Hamilton climbed very carefully down the stairs, stretching and jumping from one to the next. Fortunately, the people who had lived in the house before Bethany's family had owned a cat (Hamilton didn't even like to think about that), so there was a catflap in the back door. It locked with a bolt, but today Hamilton was lucky. Mum was using the tumble dryer, and had opened the catflap to hang the hose through. He took a run and a jump at the catflap, wriggled past the hose, and fell upside down in a snowdrift.

After the initial surprise, he turned the right way up, looked from side to side, and shook snow from his ears and whiskers. It was most useful, he thought, to have a thick warm hamster coat, but the snow on his paws was unpleasantly cold.

But never mind if his paws were cold – he wasn't going back until he'd enjoyed a bit of snow. First, he ran to the shed where Sam's rabbit, Bobby, lived. Bobby might like to play in the snow too. Hamilton darted under the shed door.

'Bobby!' he called, scratching at the hutch. 'Are you awake?'

There was a silence, then a rustling of straw and Bobby's nose was soon twitching at the wire netting.

'Oh, it's you,' he said. 'Smarty-whiskers. Awake? Course I'm awake. Been up for hours. Anything going on?'

'It's snowing!' said Hamilton, bouncing with excitement. 'Do you want to see?'

Bobby twitched an ear. 'What would I want to do that for?' he demanded.

'It's beautiful!' insisted Hamilton. Perhaps Bobby, who lived in his hutch in the shed, had never seen snow. 'Do you want to have a look? I can open your hutch for you. There are plenty of gaps in the walls for you to look through.'

'Are you kidding?' said Bobby. 'I know all

about snow. It's cold and you can't eat it. Useless.'

'But it's amazing!' said Hamilton, waving his paws as if he could magic the right word out of the air. 'It's wonderful!'

Bobby took a drink from his bottle. 'You're a bit funny, you,' he said, and sat back to wash his ears.

It was a shame. Hamilton would have liked to share the snow with someone, but Bobby wasn't interested, so he ran into the garden to play.

The snowy landscape was so magical and so confusing that he stood for a moment wondering what to do. Should he make tunnels in it, roll in it, make a snowman or throw snowballs? Should he do all of them, and if he did, which should he do first?

Rolling in it might not be a good idea, even with a fur coat, but he remembered what Bethany had said about how to make

a snowman. He made a ball about the size
of a pea, and began to push it through the
snow, over and over, watching in delight as
it grew bigger.

A ball wouldn't be the right shape for a
hamster, even a plump one, so he made a fat
snow sausage, rolled it until it was about his
own size and stood it on end with a snowball
on top. A couple of pebbles from the path
became its eyes, and it soon had whiskers of dry
grass. Its pebble nose dropped off, but
Hamilton decided that his first ever snow
hamster was a pretty good effort. He wished he
could take a photograph of it.

But now he could feel the cold creeping
through his fur. Time to get warm. Hamilton
ran to the catflap.

To his horror, Mum had finished the
tumble-drying and had put the hose away. The
catflap was closed. He pushed at it with both
paws, but it was firmly bolted. He was locked out.

Being an intelligent hamster he ran around the house looking for an open window, but he hadn't realized that people don't leave downstairs windows open on cold December days. He explored, sniffed and scrabbled at the walls, but there didn't seem to be any way into the house at all. He was running towards the front door when he discovered something new and quite astonishing about winter.

A drain near the front door had become covered with leaves, so that water from the drainpipe had overflowed on to the path and frozen. Hamilton didn't notice the ice – at least, not until his paws flew out from under him and he was whizzing forward on his tummy.

Where the patch of ice stopped, so did Hamilton. He stood up, shook his ears and thought how much fun that had been.

Sledging! That's what he'd been doing! He'd never realized that you could sledge without a sledge! But of course, he thought as he ran back for another go, humans can't. Hamsters can. We're made that way. This time, he slid on his back forwards, then on his back backwards, and on his tummy backwards, then standing up (and falling down), and balancing on one paw, then the other paw, until . . .

. . . until, all of a sudden, it wasn't fun any more. Water had seeped through his soft fur, making it heavy and chilled, and his paws hurt with cold. He might catch cold and be ill and worry Bethany, and he really didn't want to do that, especially on such an important day.

A robin suddenly hopped on to a step nearby, and it occurred to Hamilton that he might not be the only animal out in the snow. Minim, the music teacher's cat, might be out too! He'd met Minim before, and once was enough. Running close to the wall, searching all the time for a way in, he came at last to the front door again.

Door, thought Hamilton. *Simple*.

If you want to get into a house, go through the door.

If you want somebody to open the door, you ring the bell.

He stood back to take a good look. A honeysuckle was growing up the drainpipe beside the door and the woody, twirling stems would be easy to climb. From there, he could reach the doorbell, Mum would open it and his next problem would be getting in without her knowing he'd been out in the first place. He'd manage it somehow.

He took a run at the honeysuckle, scrambling from one branch to another. Normally, that would have been fun, but he was too cold to enjoy it and it was hard to grip the stems with frozen paws. *I'm a hero in one of Bethany's books*, he told himself. *I'm a polar explorer. And soon*, he thought, as he reached out towards the doorbell, *I'll be a warm, dry hamster.*

He pressed the doorbell. Nothing happened. He pressed harder. This time, the bell was so loud and startling that Hamilton lost his balance and fell helplessly from the branch. Unable to stop, he tumbled from the next branch to the next, trying to catch at anything at all. He grabbed at a twig, but it bent, swayed and snapped beneath him. With flailing paws, he dropped into the snow just as Mum opened the door.

Mum looked from side to side. She was sure she'd heard the doorbell. Had she been mistaken? The sewing machine had been making a noise. She stepped outside, and looked again. By the time she shrugged, gave up and went back into the house, Hamilton had scrambled out of the snow, slipped past her and hidden behind a waste-paper basket.

He stayed there, shivering. Mum closed the door, rubbed her cold hands and went back to her sewing. Hamilton, grateful, exhausted and almost too tired to climb, struggled slowly back to the warmth and safety of Bethany's room.

He had been looking forward to his nest with all his heart. But it seemed too hard to climb all the way up to his cage, especially when Bethany's pink fluffy slippers were warming under a radiator.

They looked soft, cosy, and so, so comfortable . . .

chapter 7

Bethany kicked off her snowy boots at the door, ran upstairs and threw her school bag into a corner. In just over an hour, she had to be back at school and getting ready for the concert.

'Hello, Hamilton –' she began, and stopped. He wasn't waiting to meet her, and the cage was unlocked –'Hamilton?'

She checked the nest box, hoping to find him in there – but there was no warm, sleepy hamster. Her hand met nothing but a cold nest. A little shiver of fear ran through her.

'Hamilton?' Bethany called anxiously, and lifted the pillows from her bed to see if he was hiding under there. No good. She looked under Wimble, but he wasn't there either. She opened cupboards, checked behind curtains and lay on the floor to look under the bed, calling his name all the time. There wasn't a squeak or a twitch of a whisker. With every second, Bethany became more worried. How could she go to the concert, not knowing where Hamilton was?

She looked down from the window, and saw that it was growing dark. Soon, the snow would freeze over. A terrible thought came to her and she sat down on the bed, pressing her face into her hands.

Oh, why had she ever told him about snow? She had told him how beautiful it was. She had taught him all about snowmen and snowball fights. He must have gone out to explore! The thought of Hamilton slowly freezing in the garden was unbearable. He could be trapped in a snowdrift, alone and squeaking for help as the air grew colder and colder. She rushed downstairs, grabbed her coat and ran outside, desperately whispering his name into corners and under bushes as the sky grew darker, and slithering on patches of ice. 'Hamilton! Please, please, Hamilton, where are you?'

Tears came to her eyes, and she brushed them away crossly. There was no time to cry. For such an intelligent animal, Hamilton didn't seem to understand danger. But, when she had rubbed her eyes, she saw that a very clear furrow ran through the snow. It was exactly hamster-size.

Bethany felt a moment of joy – *he's been here, I just have to follow this trail!* she thought. Then her heart sank again. The snow on either side of the furrow was already turning to glittering crystals of ice. Hamilton might have been out here hours ago. Was he still outside? Was he far away, lost and cold?

She walked along the furrow, then stopped, gasped and lost all hope.

Before her stood a frozen hamster.

'Hamilton!' she cried, and dropped to her knees to scoop him up. The snow hamster fell to pieces in her hands.

Something like a sob or a hiccup rose in Bethany's throat, and she found herself laughing because Hamilton had made a snow hamster, and crying because he had been out in the cold and was still missing. *Concentrate*, she told herself. *The furrow ends here. Hamilton must have built the snow hamster, and come back the same way. Turn back.*

Closer to the house, where the snow wasn't so deep and soft, Bethany could just detect a tiny trace of pawprints, and her heart began to beat more quickly. These were definitely his prints. He had come round the house, perhaps looking for a way in.

'It's as if he wanted to shelter from the snow,' she murmured to herself. 'Poor little –'

'BETHANY!' Mum appeared at the door, and Bethany jumped. 'What do you think you're doing! We have to be out in less than an hour, and you're messing about in the snow as if you had nothing to do and all day to do it in! Your tea's ready. Look at you! You're soaked to the ankles! Did you fall in the snow? Get out of those wet things before you catch pneumonia! We don't want anyone else with a cold! And quickly!'

There was no point in arguing, and the trail did look as if Hamilton might have found his way back into the house. He could be sheltering somewhere. She could only hope so. Perhaps she'd get upstairs and find that, while she'd been outside, he'd made his way back and was safely curled up in his nest box. She ran upstairs to look, but the nest box was as empty as before.

'Oh, Hamilton,' she said, and peeled off the chilly wet socks that were clinging to her ankles. 'Hamilton,' she repeated, rubbing warmth into her cold feet. She remembered that she'd left her slippers by the radiator to get warm, and gratefully slipped her right foot into her right slipper. That was much better. But she couldn't get her left slipper on at all.

She waggled her toes. Something must have got stuck in there. Something soft. Must be a pair of socks. She lifted it up to look inside, and two bright but somewhat indignant eyes looked back at her.

'Hamilton!'

Gladness ran all the way through Bethany. It washed the cold out of her, and filled her with warmth as she lifted him out.

'I was so worried about you!' she said, cradling him in her hands. 'You've been out in the snow, haven't you?' She picked him up and tried to speak sternly. 'You know it's bad for you to get cold and wet.'

Hamilton shrugged.

Bethany gave him her phone. I'M OK, he

texted. HAD FUN. MADE SNOW HMSTR. But when he looked properly at Bethany's face, he saw that her eyes were a bit pink and there were traces of tears on her face. SORRY, BETHANY, he texted, and ran up her arm to nuzzle her face.

'Don't do it again,' said Bethany. 'And I know about your snow hamster. I found it when I was looking for you.' His eyes lit up, and she decided not to tell him that it had scared her to bits and she'd accidentally wrecked it. 'Are you warm now? Do you feel ill?'

Hamilton nodded for the first question and shook his head for the second. Then, he looked purposefully back at the warm, pink slipper and pointed at it.

'You want to go back?' she asked. 'Probably the best place for you. You have a lovely sleep.'

She put him carefully back in the slipper, where he turned round a few times to make himself comfortable again.

'Bethany!' called Mum. 'Tea! Now!'

'Coming!' She came down to the warm kitchen to find Sam happily eating cheese on toast.

'My costume's gone missing,' he grinned. 'Nobody knows what's happened to it. I'll have to be a snowball in my white PE kit after all.'

Bethany looked carefully at his face. It seemed a surprising coincidence that the costume he didn't want to wear had disappeared, but there was no time to ask about it.

Bethany ate quickly, and hurried back upstairs.

'It's time to go to the concert,' she told Hamilton as he peeped out of her slipper. He sat up straight, his eyes bright and his whiskers twitching with excitement. 'Hide in my bag and be very, very good. No adventures. Don't go anywhere without telling me. I don't want anything to happen to you.'

She opened her bag so that Hamilton could run into it, and, with a sudden bright idea, popped the slipper in too. He jumped into it and disappeared. Presently, two paws appeared over the edge and Hamilton popped up, looking over the edge of the slipper as if it were a boat and he were steering it home. Careful to miss Hamilton, Bethany threw in her phone, her hairbrush and a few other odds and ends that she might want, and stepped into her shoes.

'Time to go!' called Mum.

'Ready!' Bethany called back, and read the new message on her phone.

R U NERVOUS?

'Yes', she said. 'I know we can get the song right. It's just the thought of all those people looking at me that makes me scared, but I'll be fine with Chloe there. And you, Hamilton.'

chapter 8

The school hall sparkled with tinsel, garlands and paper angels. Children swarmed everywhere, some in costumes and some in school uniform. Teachers and parents brushed hair, fastened buttons and helped small angels with their halos. Snow was falling again. A little group of the younger children pleaded to be allowed to go out to play, and were firmly told that they mustn't.

'But we made a slide at break time,' said one of them.

'Exactly,' said Mrs Strickland, Bethany's

teacher. 'That's why you're staying in. We don't want any broken legs, thank you.'

Bethany stretched up on tiptoe to see over the heads of the crowd until she saw Chloe's neat blonde head. Struggling through the masses of parents and children, they managed to meet in the middle of the hall. As her best friend came nearer, Bethany could see the frown of anxiety on Chloe's face. Her eyes and nose were pink. 'You nervous?' Bethany asked.

For a moment, Chloe said nothing. When she did speak, her voice was a hoarse whisper, so quiet that Bethany had to lower her head to hear her.

'Sorry,' she croaked. 'My voice has gone. I can hardly speak. Can't sing a note. You'll have to sing . . .' Her voice faded to nothing, but Bethany knew what the sentence would have been: 'You'll have to sing by yourself.'

Bethany's heart sank. This was terrible – she

couldn't perform by herself! But she knew she mustn't let Chloe know how disappointed she was – it wasn't Chloe's fault she was unwell, after all.

'Oh, poor Chloe,' said Bethany, and hugged her. 'I'm sorry you can't sing. You just get better.'

'Poor you,' whispered Chloe.

'Oh, don't worry about me,' said Bethany. 'I'll be OK. We'll have to tell Miss Fossett.'

But Bethany didn't feel OK at all as they went to talk to Miss Fossett. She felt sick with nerves. *I wish I'd never agreed to sing the stupid song*, she thought, as she wove her way through the hall. Her hand rested on the comforting shape of Hamilton in her bag.

Bethany soon saw that they weren't the only ones waiting for Miss Fossett. A crowd of small children pressed around her, all asking questions and wanting help with their costumes. Parents queued with questions to ask. And there, on the stage, lay something that looked like an enormous white doughnut, or sparkly mashed potato.

Someone was tugging at her sleeve, and she looked down to see Sam. His mouth was tight, and his face pale with anger.

'That's my costume!' he growled. 'That stupid white thing!'

'I thought you said it was lost!' said Bethany.

'It was,' he muttered. 'They found it.'

'Pity,' she said. 'Where did they find it?'

'Ar . . . cud,' he mumbled.

'Where?'

'Art cupboard,' he said. 'The one in my classroom.'

'Oh, I see,' said Bethany. If Sam was going to hide things, he'd have to think of somewhere better than the art cupboard. 'You can't possibly do your somersaults in that,' she said.

'I know,' said Sam. 'I wish I could just lose it properly again without anybody noticing.'

He slumped into an angry silence, and Bethany

couldn't think of anything to make him feel better. It was difficult to think about anything but the fact she had to sing by herself now. Her hands shook and she felt a bit sick, so she slipped her hand into her bag, reaching for Hamilton.

He wasn't there.

For a moment, Bethany couldn't breathe. Shaking, her hand closed on the cool, smooth shape of her phone, and she read the text.

BUSY. C U SOON. DON'T WORRY. H.

Not again! thought Bethany. She wasn't often cross with Hamilton, but hadn't she told him not to go anywhere this evening?

'All mobile phones switched off!' called Miss Fossett, looking over at her, but then she caught sight of Bethany's face, and left the parents to talk to her. 'Bethany, what's the matter? You're not ill, too, are you? Chloe doesn't look at all well.'

'No, Miss,' said Bethany. 'It's just . . . it's just that Chloe can't sing tonight. She hasn't any voice at all, and, please, Miss, I can't do it alone with all those people staring at me!'

'Now, Bethany, Chloe being ill is no excuse,' exclaimed Miss Fossett. 'Just imagine that they're not staring at you at all. Think of something happy and take a few deep breaths. I will be most disappointed if you don't sing tonight. And if you do, you can be very proud of yourself, and your family will be proud of you too. You can do it.'

Bethany thought of the afternoons she'd spent practising with Chloe, with Hamilton conducting and guiding her. She thought of Chloe, who would blame herself for being ill if Bethany didn't sing alone, and of her parents, who had looked forward to this.

Hamilton had looked forward to it, too. He'd be so disappointed if she didn't sing. For Hamilton – wherever he had got to! – and for Chloe, she must forget about all those people, and concentrate on every note and every word instead. She would sing her sweetest and best. She took a few deep breaths, and softly sang a few bars to herself to make sure that the song was still in her head.

'OK, Miss,' she said.

'Brave girl,' said Miss Fossett. 'Now, I have to make sure the Year Threes are ready.'

Bethany brushed her hair and worked her way back towards the stage, glancing from side to side in the hope of catching a glimpse of Hamilton. Parents were taking their seats and leafing through their programmes. Children were in organized groups of stars, angels, snowflakes, robins and carol singers. She slipped her hand into her pocket, hoping desperately that Hamilton might have jumped back in without her noticing, but there was nothing there except a tissue and a pound coin.

Hamilton! Please! she thought. *Where are you?*

chapter 9

Bethany was suddenly distracted from her
search for Hamilton by the sound of gasps of
surprise coming from the stage.

She worked her way through the crowd to
see Miss Fossett standing in front of the stage
holding all that was left of Sam's costume. Bits
of fluff floated to the floor. A steady trickle of
polystyrene pellets fell from one corner.
Stuffing bulged from a torn seam. Loose threads
trailed down. A button dropped off and landed
on the floor with a ping.

From the corner of her eye, Bethany saw

Sam trying not to grin and failing. Miss Fossett turned to him with her eyebrows raised.

'Miss, I don't know what happened,' he said, still unable to keep the smile off his face. 'It wasn't me.'

'He's been with me all the time,' said Mum. 'It really wasn't anything to do with Sam. Do you get mice in here?'

'Certainly not!' said Miss Fossett.

But you might have a hamster, Bethany thought. She pressed her hands to her mouth to hide her smile.

'Maybe it was already damaged, and we didn't notice,' said Miss Fossett. 'That must be it. We definitely don't have any rodents in here.'

Miss Fossett turned to Sam.

'Well, Sam, I'm most disappointed,' she said. 'As it is, you'll just have to change into . . .'

'My white PE kit?' suggested Sam helpfully.

'That'll have to do,' she sighed. 'Run and get changed.'

Sam exchanged a quick high five with Bethany while Miss Fossett wasn't looking. Then he dashed away before Miss Fossett could think of something else silly for him to wear.

'I'll help you tidy up the mess, Miss!' said Bethany, and she quickly gathered together the scraps of Sam's wrecked costume. Hamilton must be in there somewhere.

Hamilton had just discovered how much fun Christmas concerts could be. He'd not only solved Sam's problem, but he now had a supply of snowflakes that would make the most spectacular Christmas Bethany had ever seen. With his pouches crammed with fluff, and stuffing on top of his head, he looked out from the remains of Sam's costume that Bethany was clutching, waved a paw at her and ducked down again.

'I'll put this in the classroom bin, Miss,' she said over her shoulder. 'I'll only be a minute.'

'It's all right now,' Bethany whispered at the

pile of scraps in her arms. She went into the nearest classroom and closed the door. 'There's nobody else here.' Hamilton popped up, looking very pleased with himself and cleaning glitter from his whiskers. 'Hamilton, I was very worried about you! I didn't know where you were!'

Hamilton tucked his head down on his chest and looked up sheepishly at her, as if apologizing. But he knew she wasn't really cross, and she knew he wasn't really sorry. It didn't seem to matter.

'All the same,' she said, 'Sam's so happy! You're brilliant.'

Hamilton nodded. He couldn't help it – it was true, after all. And he'd enjoyed chewing up that costume.

Bethany was about to throw the fluff in the bin, when Hamilton folded his claws tightly round her finger and shook his head. He needed that!

'You want to keep it?' she said. 'OK. I suppose you want to nest in it.' She stuffed the bits of costume into her bag, and Hamilton wriggled down among them.

'We have to go into the hall now,' said Bethany, 'so I'll have to turn the phone off soon. The concert starts in five minutes.'

The destruction of Sam's costume had taken her mind off the concert for a moment. But as she thought of the waiting audience and the stage, fear trickled through her again.

'Oh, Hamilton,' she said, and stroked him. 'I'm so scared! You heard about Chloe losing her voice?'

Hamilton nodded.

'I said I'd sing by myself,' she went on. 'But I'm terrified. It was all right when there were two of us. I'll be all by myself, with all those people – all of them, and only one of me! I feel ill just thinking about it!'

Hamilton ran up her arm and rubbed his face against hers. She tried to hold him, but he ran back to the phone.

I'LL COME WITH U IN YR POCKET IF U LIKE, he offered.

For a moment, Bethany hesitated. He'd already had two adventures that day, and worried her sick both times. But at least, with Hamilton in her pocket, she'd know where he was and then she wouldn't feel so alone on stage.

'Yes, please,' she said. 'I'll feel much better with you in my pocket.' Feeling a bit better already, Bethany switched off the phone and walked back into the hall, past the rows of snowflakes and robins, to her seat beside the stage.

'Bethany,' said Miss Fossett. 'What do you have in your pocket? It's bulging!'

'I've got a packet of tissues in it, Miss,' she said, and didn't mention that she had a hamster in there, too. 'Just in case I'm catching Chloe's cold.'

'I hope you're not!' said Miss Fossett.

The Year Three choir sang. Somebody read a poem. The snowballing children did their dance, with Sam in his white shorts and T-shirt rolling, somersaulting and tumbling with a huge smile on his face, but Bethany couldn't quite enjoy it. Her moment was coming closer, and anxiety gnawed at her stomach. She took deep breaths. The robins danced, then the recorder group played their carol suite, while in Bethany's pocket, Hamilton tapped out the rhythm with a claw – then it was her turn. She stood up.

'It's you and me, Hamilton,' she whispered.

The light on the stage was bright, and the audience sat in darkness. That helped. She couldn't see the faces clearly. At the back of the hall, above the heads of the audience, was a clock with silver Christmas angels around it.

Miss Fossett sat ready at the piano. With her hands folded in front of her, Bethany could feel the edge of her pocket against her wrist, and reminded herself that Hamilton was in there. She nodded at Miss Fossett, who gave her the first note, then fixed her eyes on the topmost angel and began to sing.

'How far is it to Bethlehem? Not very far.
Shall we find the stable room, lit by a star?'

She listened to the piano and to her own voice as she sang, keeping in time and staying in tune. The first three lines were over, then the first verse. She was concentrating so hard that in a moment of blank panic she realized she'd forgotten the next line – *Oh, help – it's something to do with babies – rhymes with 'sheep'. Oh, yes . . .*

'May we peep like them and see Jesus asleep?'

But that moment had shaken her confidence. *They all noticed*, she thought. *I came in a tiny bit late and they must have noticed*. Her throat tightened and her voice wasn't as strong as it had been. *Pull yourself together, Bethany*, she told herself. She sang on.

'Will he know we've come so far, just for his sake?'

But Hamilton had heard that quaver in her voice. Bethany needed his help. *It was all right when there were two of us*. That's what she'd said. He had an idea.

Still singing, Bethany slipped her hand into her pocket to calm Hamilton, who seemed to be trying to get out. He ran up her arm and on to her shoulder.

'Ooh!' said all the audience. There was a rustle as everyone leant forward to look, and Bethany knew at once what Hamilton was doing. All eyes were on him now. Nobody was looking at her any more. She smiled in her song, remembering that she had told Hamilton she would sing for him. She lifted him down from her shoulder and held him on the palm of her hand, level with her face, as she sang in her strongest voice:

'*For all weary children . . .*'

When her last note faded, there was a silence that seemed to last for hours, so Bethany didn't know what to do next. Then the applause and cheering began, and Bethany bowed, holding Hamilton before her in her cupped hands. Hamilton nearly bowed too, but remembered just in time that this might give away his secret – so he stood still in Bethany's hands and hoped that he looked ordinary. He didn't even wave as Bethany walked back to her place, held him to her cheek and whispered, 'You star!'

The children in the Nativity play trooped

on to the stage to take their places, straining on tiptoe and tripping over their costumes as they tried to see if Hamilton was still there. But Bethany had slipped him quietly back into her pocket.

At the end of the concert, friends and family clustered round Bethany. Everyone wanted to know how she had trained the hamster, and why she hadn't told anyone about bringing him to the concert. Children were asking if they could teach their hamsters to do that. Chloe hugged her, and asked her, in a raspy whisper, why she hadn't let her in on the secret.

'I didn't mean it to happen like that,' Bethany whispered back. 'I brought him because I was nervous. Hamilton did the rest.'

'Well done, Hammy,' said Chloe. Bethany and Hamilton exchanged glances. Hammy! It wasn't much better than Fluffpot.

Parents were gathering their children and taking them home. As they walked out to the car park, everyone was talking about That Hamster.

Tim Taverner had been working late that evening. He had taken to driving home at night by way of Spinhill, where Bethany and Chloe lived, and past the school. Always, his tracking device was switched on, just in case the hamster was anywhere near. One day, he might just get the chance to snatch it.

He had almost driven past the school when he saw that the lights were on, and people were leaving. There must be something happening there this evening – some sort of Christmas do. He wasn't sure which school Bethany and Chloe went to, but this one seemed likely. He parked outside the school gates (which wasn't allowed) and wound down the window to hear what people were saying as they walked away.

'Brilliant concert,' said one. 'That hamster!'
Tim squeaked, and jumped in his seat.

'Mum, can I have a hamster?' said a child.

'However did she train it?' wondered someone out loud. 'It was as good as gold.'

'It can't have been a real one,' said someone else. 'It must have had batteries.'

With shaking hands, Tim opened the glovebox and took out the tracking device. There was no signal, but that might just mean that something was blocking it, or that he wasn't quite near enough yet. If the microspecked hamster had been in the school, it might still be there. Hastily, he got out of the car and strode through the school gates.

What made it harder for him was that, while everybody else was trying to get out of the school, Tim was desperate to get in. He struggled through the crowds, weaving and elbowing his way with mutters of 'Excuse me', and 'I need to get through'. It was almost impossible, so he'd have to go round the crowds, not through them.

'Careful,' called a teacher. 'There's a . . .'

Tim's feet slid away from under him.

'. . . slippery patch there,' finished the teacher, as Tim fell and sped backwards across the ice towards the open gate. People rushed to help, but Tim was travelling much faster than they were, and beyond the gate was the main road.

It was a good thing that Tim had parked his car at the school gates (which was absolutely not allowed), because it gave him something to crash into. In only a few seconds he had remembered who he was and where he was. After that he soon worked out which way was up, so he rubbed his head and tried to stand. It wasn't easy, because the crowd had finally caught up and gathered about him. A lot of people were talking at once, saying things like, 'Keep down now, keep your head down' and 'Are you hurt?' and 'Do you feel faint?'

Tim put his hand to the back of his head. He

had hit it against the car, not hard enough to knock himself out, but enough to hurt and make him a bit dizzy. It was hard to concentrate.

'He's banged his head,' said someone. 'That could be serious. I'm calling an ambulance.'

'Don't need one,' muttered Tim.

'Yes, you do,' said a woman with a phone in her hand. 'You need to see a doctor.'

'I am a doctor,' said Tim.

'He thinks he's a doctor,' said the woman with the phone. 'He's definitely not well.'

'Maybe he really is a doctor,' said someone else, and knelt beside Tim. 'Are you a doctor, love?'

'Not that sort of doctor,' said Tim, still struggling and failing to get up. He tried to say that he had a doctorate in applied artificial intelligence, but it was too hard. 'I'm another kind of doctor.'

'Is he Doctor Who?' asked a little boy excitedly. 'Mum, is he Doctor Who?'

Tim struggled to remember what he was

looking for. 'Hamster,' he said. 'Micro . . . thing . . .' and when the ambulance arrived, the bystanders were ready to explain that he'd had a nasty bang on the head and thought his name was Dr Hamster. They said he'd probably got hamsters into his head because he'd heard them talking about the one in the school concert.

'Come with us to hospital, sir,' said the ambulance driver kindly, some minutes later. 'We'll get you checked over. Is there anyone we should phone for you?'

By the time Tim arrived at hospital, Bethany, Sam and their mum and dad were sitting round the kitchen table, drinking hot chocolate and talking about the concert. Hamilton sat on Bethany's lap, eating a piece of apple and looking as innocent as a hamster can.

'Sam, your somersaults were brilliant,' said Bethany.

'Thank you. I can't believe I didn't have to

wear that stupid costume in the end! How
brilliant is that? I wonder how it happened . . .'
he said.

Bethany glanced down at Hamilton with a
smile.

'Hamilton was so good!' said Mum.

'So was Bethany,' said Dad.

'Oh, yes, but I knew she'd be good,' said
Mum. 'How did you teach him to do that?'

'I didn't,' said Bethany, stroking Hamilton.
'He just did it by himself.'

'But he was in your pocket!' said Dad. 'You
must have put him in there.'

'I suppose so,' said Bethany, looking
wide-eyed and innocent as if she had no idea
how he got there.

'I'm amazed that he didn't run away,' said Dad.

'But why would he?' asked Bethany, with a
daydreamy look. 'He likes being with me.'

'I'm going to build a snowman in the
morning,' said Sam.

'It might be your last chance,' said Dad. 'The forecast says the snow won't last much longer.'

Later that night, when Bethany and Hamilton were still sitting at her bedroom window, wrapped in her duvet and looking at the last of the snow and the stars, Tim Taverner's parents arrived at the hospital.

'He's a bit confused, but we haven't found any serious damage,' the doctor told them. 'But he says he lives alone, so we can't send him home yet. He needs to be with other people, just in case there are any after-effects from that head injury.'

'He's coming home with us,' said Mrs Taverner firmly. 'He was due to come home soon anyway for Christmas. It's the best place for him to be.'

'Absolutely,' agreed the doctor. 'If he falls asleep a lot, gets drowsy, vomits or behaves strangely, take him to the nearest hospital.

Lucky you, Dr Taverner! A few extra days with your mum looking after you!'

So Tim was taken to his parents' house, where his mother regularly checked him to see if he was falling asleep and asked him if he was feeling all right. When old friends and relations called, Tim had to meet them and listen to their boring conversations about Brussels sprouts and what was on the telly this year. There was a computer at his parents' house, but they wouldn't let him use it while he was recovering and on holiday. So, unable to do any hamster tracking whatsoever, Tim played chess against his father and Scrabble against himself.

He even helped his mum.

chapter 10

On Christmas Eve, while Hamilton was asleep,
Bethany finished the picture she was drawing as
a present for him, and pegged it to his nest box.
When that was in place, she made a tiny red
stocking and stuffed it with pieces of apple,
sultanas and all his favourite things. That was to
hang on his wheel. Her own stocking – one of
her welly boot socks – was already hanging on
the door. And, as she was falling asleep,
Hamilton was just waking up.

He let himself out of his cage and sat up at
the window, too excited to notice anything

different about his cage. As the forecast had
said, the snow had melted a few days before,
and only a grubby white mound remained
where Bethany and Sam had built a snowman.

Hamilton didn't mind. It made his surprise
even better. First, he took out all the fluffy bits
of stuffing, tissues and cotton wool he had been
storing in his nest box, shook off the sawdust,
then set to work digging out all the secret stores
of Bethany's snow.

By the time he'd stored it all away he had
several little snow mounds at various points in
Bethany's room. There were nibbled bits of
fabric behind the radiator, glitter from the
Christmas decorations under a corner of the
carpet, a whole suitcase full of snow on top of
the wardrobe and the shredded remains of
Sam's costume, which he had managed to hide
in the box of toys that Bethany never played
with any more. It came to thousands and
thousands of snowflakes.

He spread Bethany's snow over the bookshelf, the desk and the windowsill. Feathers and scraps from the waste paper were scattered over her bed until the whole room looked like a perfect winter landscape. All he had to do now was assemble his snowstorm by rearranging his hoard on the wardrobe. Bethany had hung garlands and tinsel about the room, which were very useful for climbing, but all that running about left Hamilton very tired by the time he'd finished.

He yawned, and looked at the clock. There was plenty of time for a chapter or two of story before bed. He hadn't started *A Christmas Carol* yet, and he liked books by Charles Dickens.

Bethany kept her phone and a small torch on the table beside her bed. He set the timer on the phone to give her a wake-up call, changed the ring tone to something more suitable for Christmas and texted a message for her for when she woke up. Then he heaved *A Christmas*

Carol from the shelf (dislodging a few feather snowflakes as he did so), found his place and switched on the torch using both front paws and his teeth. He curled up beside Bethany and read until he fell asleep.

Bethany was woken on Christmas morning by the sound of her mobile phone playing 'Hark the Herald Angels Sing'. She sat up, rubbing her eyes and yawning as she picked up her phone, not noticing that beside her, Hamilton was yawning and rubbing his eyes, too. She picked up the phone and read the text – HPPY CHRMAS BETHANY LOVE FR HAMILTON.

'Thank you, Hamilton!' she said, and felt a tickle against her hand as he climbed into her palm. 'Happy Christmas to you too!' She switched on the light, and gasped.

'Snow!' she cried. 'It's snow!'

She pushed her hands into the layer of white on her bed. Snow – or something very like it – covered every surface. As she sat up, a snowfall drifted on to the floor.

'It's magical!' she exclaimed. 'Hamilton, did you do . . . Hamilton, where have you gone?'

The answer came in a cloud of snowflakes cascading from the wardrobe. Hamilton jumped down with them, scampered over the bed and threw pawfuls of snow at her before jumping on to the phone.

WARM SNOW! he texted with pride.

'It's wonderful!' she laughed, and threw a snow shower high into the air so it fell around her. 'What a perfect present! And, Hamilton, the best thing is we won't even have to tidy it up because nobody comes in here on Christmas Day. Everyone's too busy, what with presents, and church, and Granny Elliott and dinner. They'll just play with the presents or fall asleep, and we'll come up here and play with the snow for as long as we want.' She jumped out of bed and threw feathers over him. 'You must have worked so hard! You really are amazing!'

For a moment, she looked a little less happy. 'All I've done for you is your stocking,' she said sadly, 'and a –'

At the word 'stocking', Hamilton's ears twitched. He hadn't realized that hamsters had stockings! He looked round, saw the tiny red stocking hanging from his wheel, and dashed in delight to bite through the thread holding it up. Out fell a tiny paper aeroplane, followed by a banquet of fruit and seeds. Bethany scrambled to the end of her bed and lifted down her own stocking – a heavy, lumpy welly sock. 'I'm going to Mum and Dad's room to open this,' she said. 'Want to come with me?'

Hamilton looked at Bethany's stocking, blinked and looked again. Astonishing! He'd been busy all last night, and had slept on Bethany's pillow. Surely he would have noticed somebody putting it there? He watched,

fascinated, as she unloaded its contents on to
Mum and Dad's bed. There were sweets in
there, satsumas, money, pens and pencils, a
comb, a sugar mouse and a tiny cuddly dog.
Christmas really was amazing!

All afternoon, Bethany and Hamilton played
with the pretend snow, and before Bethany
went to bed they piled it up into a snowman.
He had to be packed into a pillowcase to keep
him from falling apart, and Bethany tied a
length of Christmas ribbon round where his
neck should be to shape his head. She knew
better than to offer Hamilton a ribbon. It would
have been undignified.

'And I've got one more present for you,' she
said. This was a very special surprise, and she had
looked forward all afternoon to this moment,
ever since they pulled crackers after lunch. 'Look
what I got in my cracker! It's for you!'

She opened her hand. There lay a packet of
tiny – very tiny – hamster-sized screwdrivers.

He gazed up at her with shining eyes, and there was no need to ask for the phone. His delighted look and the way he rubbed his face on her hand said all he needed to say.

'That snow was my best ever Christmas present,' she said, as she wriggled into bed that night and opened *A Christmas Carol*. Hamilton ran back into his cage, used one of his new screwdrivers to adjust the wheel, had a little run, then popped a few sultanas into his pouches, so he'd have something to eat during bedtime reading. Today had been a great success. Warm snow was a truly wonderful invention.

With sultanas bulging in his cheeks, he turned to run back to Bethany when something caught his eye. There was another present in his cage! For the first time, he noticed the picture Bethany had fastened to the nest box, and turned to take a good look at it.

It was a beautiful drawing of the Nativity scene. Tiny though it was, he could see Mary,

Joseph and Jesus, with the animals and an angel. Perhaps there hadn't been room for shepherds and kings, but that didn't matter at all. On the edge of the manger, standing upright in the straw, was a small, fluffy, white and gold hamster.

I knew it, thought Hamilton. *There had to be a hamster!*

HAMMY'S TOP TEN CHRISTMAS TIPS

 1 You wouldn't believe how much food people have around the house at Christmas! You'll find plenty of **nuts**, **fruit** and **crumbs**. Remember what your pouches are for!

 2 I love **warm snow**. Real snow could seriously damage your health, not to mention your whiskers.

 3 If your person forgets to **clean your cage** at Christmas, you'll have to remind them. Stand on your hind legs, hold the bars with your front paws and do **THE LOOK**. You know the one I mean.

 4 **Father Christmas** doesn't mind hamsters spotting him. If you're having a **night run** on Christmas Eve, you may be surprised!

5 If your person leaves a **carrot** lying around on Christmas Eve, it's for the reindeer. **Don't eat it!**

6 If your person draws a picture of the **nativity scene**, make sure they add a hamster!

7 Get dancing to all the **Christmas tunes**! It's fun and works off all those Christmas nibbles.

8 **Paper decorations** look fantastic, especially in your cage (or apartment, as I prefer to think of it.)

9 **Fluff up your fur** so you look your best for Christmas. Your person will love it.

10 There's a funny Christmas song called *The Twelve Days of Christmas*. See if you and your person can change it so that you can get as many hamsters in as possible, like this:

> On the third day of Christmas my true love sent to me,
> Three French hamsters,
> Two turtle hamsters,
> And a hamster in a pear tree!

Have fun, and Happy Christmas!

Hamilton

HAMMY'S FAVOURITE CHRISTMAS GIFTS!

⭐ **AN AEROPLANE BOOK**
(Because one day, hamsters will take to the sky.)

⭐ **A MOBILE PHONE**
(For typing out all the very important things your person needs to know.)

⭐ **A NEW CROSSWORD/SUDOKU BOOK**
(Work your way through it. Or chew your way through it, if you don't like puzzles.)

⭐ **CARDBOARD TUBES**
(Great for tunnelling in and you can nibble them too. Kitchen rolls are best. The ones from Christmas crackers could make you ill, and as for loo rolls – don't even think about it!)

THE LATEST DESIGN OF HAMSTER WHEELS
(For going round and round and round . . . as you do.)

A SUPER-DELUXE APARTMENT
(Your person may call it a cage.)

A FLUFFY SLIPPER
(Perfect for curling up in. If your person gets new ones for Christmas, you might get the old ones!)

A NICE CHUNK OF WOOD TO GNAW ON
(Your person has to make sure it's a kind that's safe to eat. Apple-wood is best. Anybody got an apple tree?)

ENOUGH FRUIT TO FIT COMFORTABLY IN THE CHEEKS
(No explanation needed!)

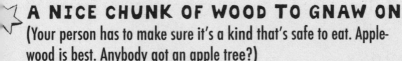

SNOW! WARM SNOW!
(It wouldn't be Christmas without it, and it makes Bethany smile.)

HAMMY'S CHRISTMAS CROSSWORD

ACROSS

4 Hamilton has these instead of feet. Much better for climbing up cupboards.

6 Hamilton's rabbit friend.

7 A long, sparkly Christmas decoration.

8 Where the baby Jesus slept.

9 A fun winter sport that even Hamilton can do on his stomach.

10 This Christmas toy makes a big bang.

12 Hamilton has made it his mission to collect as many of these as possible for Bethany.

13 Chloe's favourite nickname for Hamilton.

DOWN

1 Bethany has to sing one of these in the Christmas play.

2 What Hamilton sends to get messages to Bethany.

3 The best fluffy animal ever!

4 A delicious Christmas dessert that looks like a brown stone with white paint poured over it.

5 A big round person made of snow.

9 Hang this at the end of your bed on Christmas Eve and see how many gifts you get the next morning . . .

11 Hamilton loves running round on this!

12 This animal pulls Santas's sleigh and is much bigger than a hamster.